The William Shakespeare

CHILDREN'S COLLECTION

Dados Internacionais de Catalogação na Publicação (CIP) de acordo com ISBD

S5271k Shakespeare, William
King Lear / William Shakespeare. - Jandira, SP : W. Books, 2025.
96 p. ; 12,80cm x 19,80cm. - (Classics).

ISBN: 978-65-5294-198-5

1. Literatura inglesa. 2. Clássicos. 3. Aventura. 4. Fantasia. 5. Imaginação. I. Título. II. Série.

2025-2515 CDD 823
CDU 821.111

Elaborada por Lucio Feitosa - CRB-8/8803
Índice para catálogo sistemático:
1. Literatura inglesa 823
2. Literatura inglesa 821.111-3

Text based on the original play by William Shakespeare,
adapted by Gemma Barder
Illustrations by Mai Ngo

1st edition in 2025
www.cirandacultural.com.br

EASY CLASSICS

William Shakespeare

King Lear

W. Books

King Lear
King of England

Duke of Kent
King Lear's oldest friend

Goneril, Regan and Cordelia
King Lear's daughters

Duke of Albany

Goneril's husband

Duke of Cornwall

Regan's husband

The Jester

The king's entertainer

King of France

Cordelia's husband

Chapter One

King Lear sat in his throne room, listening to the rain bounce off the window. He sighed heavily, feeling an ache in his back as he shifted on his grand red and gold chair.

'What has happened to the young, heroic king I once was?' Lear asked out loud.

The king's oldest friend, the Duke of Kent, was placing a

log on the fire, trying to keep out the cold. He smiled at the king's question.

'He grew into a wise and beloved leader,' replied Kent.

'Wise and *old*,' said Lear, standing and rubbing his back. 'I have ruled England for so long. I am tired, my friend.'

The only other person in

the room was the jester, an entertainer who played music and told jokes to keep the king amused.

'What do you say, Jester?' said Lear. 'Am I a broken-down old man?'

The jester danced his way over to the king. 'Let me check, Your Majesty!' The jester skipped around the king, prodding him and looking into his ear.

He was the only person in the whole country who could get away with such behaviour. The king laughed, and then he shooed the jester away.

'Alas! Your attempt to make me feel better has not entirely worked,' said Lear. 'Kent, I have an idea.'

The Duke of Kent stepped closer, eager to hear what the king was going to say.

'I have decided that I want to step down as king and pass the kingdom of England to my three daughters,' Lear began. 'I will have to divide the country into three equal parts so that they each have land and people to rule over.'

Kent was taken aback by the news. 'Are you certain, Your Majesty?' he asked. 'For one thing, the country *cannot* be divided equally. Some parts of the country are far richer than others. How will you decide which of your daughters deserves the richest part?'

The king took a deep breath, pondering the question.

'Simple! I shall ask each of them how much they love me,' replied

Lear. 'Whoever loves me the most will get the richest part of the country to rule over.'

Kent frowned. The king's plan seemed foolish to him. He wanted to decide the future of England by how much each of his daughters loved him, rather than which daughter was the most capable and loyal leader. Kent had been worried for some time that the king was not himself. His actions and decisions had become

capable

Having the skill or power to do what is needed.

stranger and stranger over the past few years, and now this. It was the *strangest* idea of all.

'A marvellous idea!' sang the jester. 'A stupendous idea!

What could possibly go wrong?'

Kent glared at the jester, wishing he would go away.

'Your Majesty, are you sure?' Kent asked at last. 'Perhaps if we took a bit more time to think about it, we could–'

'No!' the king shouted, growing frustrated with his friend. 'The time for thinking is over. Summon Goneril, Regan and Cordelia to me at once. I have made my decision.'

summon

To call a person or group to appear for a particular purpose.

Chapter Two

The Duke of Kent did as he was asked. He sent one messenger to Goneril's home where she lived with her husband, The Duke of Albany, and another to Regan's home where she lived with her husband, the Duke of Cornwall.

King Lear's youngest daughter, Cordelia, still lived with him. However, it would not be long before she too would be leaving her childhood home. The noble and handsome King of France had fallen in love with Cordelia, and their engagement was shortly to be announced to the country. However, the king had his own announcement to make first.

Within a few days, the castle was full of visitors.

'Family, friends,' King Lear

began, as he stood in front of his daughters, their families and his trusted advisors. 'I have had the pleasure of ruling over this great country for a long time and I shall cherish these years dearly.

However, I am tired and I want the people to be guided by new rulers. People who I can trust. So, from this day on, I am dividing England into three parts. Each part is to be ruled by one of my daughters.'

Goneril and Regan stared at each other in sheer delight. They both stepped forward, eager to receive their new lands and riches. But Cordelia looked confused. She glanced at the Duke of Kent, who she knew was her father's closest friend, and saw that he looked just as worried.

'Now, in order to decide which part of the country goes to which daughter, I ask each of you to come here and declare your love for me.' Lear held out his hand, waiting for his eldest daughter to take it. Goneril stepped forward.

'Dearest Father,' she began, kneeling at the king's feet. 'I love you more than words can say. More than life itself!'

The king smiled with satisfaction and let Goneril's hand go. Goneril turned and winked at her husband, proud of herself for doing a good job of convincing her father that she loved him best.

Next, Regan stepped forward. She threw her arms around the king and began to sob (although curiously no tears fell from her eyes).

'Oh Papa!' she said. 'Just thinking about how much I love you makes me overcome with emotion. You are the light in my life. I love you more than there are stars in the sky.'

The king chuckled, patting his daughter on the back. 'Well, well,' he said. 'That is a fine declaration!'

Regan gave a satisfied smile to her sisters, feeling as though she had already won.

'I can't do this,' Cordelia whispered to the King of France. 'Not in front of all these people!'

'Do you not love your father?' questioned the King of France.

'Of course I do,' Cordelia replied. 'Very much.'

'Then you must try.'

Chapter Three

Cordelia felt nervous to be making such a private gesture in front of a large crowd. She approached the throne and curtseyed before her father.

'Well then, child, what do you have to say?' asked Lear.

Cordelia looked at her feet. 'I-I can't!' she stuttered, her face flushing red.

'If you do not speak, then how will I know how much you love me?'

Cordelia looked into her father's eyes. Eventually, she summoned up the courage to speak.

'Father, I do love you, but I do not have the words to describe it to you,' she began. 'But my love for you is true and real.'

King Lear took a step back. He stared at Cordelia with a look of confusion and disgust on his face.

'Is that all you have to say to me?' he retorted. Cordelia nodded. 'I see. Then it is clear who my real, loving daughters are and who does not care for me at all!'

Lear's face slowly turned red. He balled his hands into fists with fury. Instinctively, the King of France took a step forward and placed a protective hand on Cordelia's shoulder.

'Goneril and Regan will rule over half of the country each!' Lear spat. 'And *you*!' he pointed a trembling finger at Cordelia. 'You can leave this place and never come back! It would have been better if you had not been born!'

Cordelia's heart felt as though it had been shattered into thousands of pieces. Her eyes filled with tears as the Duke of Kent tried to intervene.

'Your Majesty, I am sure Cordelia loves you just as much as Goneril and Regan,' he began. 'But she has always been shy.'

intervene

To enter a situation in order to try and change what is happening.

King Lear furiously turned to meet his friend.

'If you believe that, you do not love me either!' he said. King Lear turned to look at the King of France as he continued, 'I am sorry, Your Highness, it seems you are engaged to an un-loving, ungrateful woman. I would not blame you if you wanted to call off the wedding.'

The King of France gently took Cordelia's trembling hand.

'That will not happen,' he began. 'In fact, her honesty makes me love her even more. If you do not want *your* daughter here, then I shall take her back to France with me this very day.'

Cordelia stood still, staring at her father in shock. The room had fallen silent.

Her elder sisters were grinning greedily, waiting to take over the country, with their husbands by their side. Cordelia said nothing and let herself be guided away by the King of France, out of the castle and out of the country.

The Duke of Kent watched Cordelia go, unsure what to do next.

'Your Majesty, please,' he said, looking at the faces of the stunned crowd, then back to Lear.

'What are you still doing here, Kent?' Lear said, his face still red with anger. 'You are hereby banished from England. I wish to never see your face again.'

banish

To order somebody to leave a place, especially a country, as a punishment.

Chapter Four

Once the Duke of Kent's lonely retreating footsteps could no longer be heard, King Lear clapped his hands together in joy.

'Now then!' he said, turning to his remaining daughters. 'Goneril and Regan, you are now in charge of England. All I ask is for one hundred knights to protect me, a

knight
A man of high social position trained to fight as a soldier on a horse.

servant to help me and my loyal jester to entertain me.'

'Oh Father, that sounds wonderful!' said Goneril, smiling and batting her eyelashes at her father.

'Simply marvellous,' agreed Regan. 'Why, you are *so* clever to have worked all this out!'

The old king could not see that his greedy daughters did not think he was clever at all. At that moment, all they cared about

was getting their hands on the land and riches their father had promised to them.

'Now that I am retired,' continued Lear, 'I will divide my time between the daughters who love me so well. I will live half of the time with you, Goneril, and the other half with you, Regan.'

The smile on Goneril and Regan's faces faded. It was true that they wanted their father's land and castles, but they did not, in any way at all, actually want *him*.

Once the declaration was over, the crowd of invited guests made their farewells and returned to their homes. Over the coming weeks, the news of Lear's retirement slowly and steadily began to travel across the country.

Immediately after the guests had left, Goneril quickly made her way through the corridors of the castle. She found the room Regan and the Duke of Cornwall were staying in that night. There was something she wanted to do before returning home.

Goneril knocked on the heavy wooden door. 'Sister?' she

whispered. 'Sister, are you awake?'

The door to Regan's room creaked open and Goneril slipped inside. She found Regan pacing back and forth in front of her bedroom fire.

'Did you hear what the old fool said?' Goneril said. 'He wants to live with us! He is bound to interfere with how we decide to rule over our parts of England. Father won't be able to stop himself!'

Regan halted her pacing and looked at Goneril.

'Then we must *find* a way to stop him,' Regan said. 'It should not be too difficult. After all, he is clearly not in his right mind.'

‘What do you mean?’ asked Goneril.

‘We both know he loved Cordelia more than us,’ Regan said. ‘And yet he still banished her from the country! He is not in his right mind, which means we will be able to overpower him easily and share the country between us without his meddling.’

Goneril thought for a moment, then she met her sister’s gaze with a smile.

‘Do you know what, sister,’ she said. ‘I think you just might be right.’

Chapter Five

Cordelia strolled in the gardens of her grand palace in Paris. It was a beautiful spring day and the air was filled with the scent of her husband's favourite roses. It had been months since that awful day when her father had banished her from England. During that time, she had married the King of France and settled into her new country.

Although she felt safe and loved in her new home, not a day went by that she did not think of her father, or how her elder sisters were now ruling England in his place.

'Your Majesty!' called a familiar voice. Cordelia turned to see the Duke of Kent hurrying towards her from the palace. Since he had

been banished on the same day as Cordelia, and for the crime of defending her, Cordelia had offered him a home with her at the palace.

'Forgive me for intruding on your walk,' said Kent, a little out of breath. 'I have had news from England.' He held up a sheet of parchment with a broken wax seal. 'My friends tell me that all is not well. Since your sisters took over from your father, they have not been good rulers. They have increased taxes. They are selfish and greedy and do not think of the people at all.'

Cordelia sighed. 'I was afraid that might happen,' she said. 'My sisters never cared about the people of England. They only

parchment

A material like paper made of the skins of sheep or goats.

tax

Money paid by people of a country to the government.

cared about the money, castles and land they would get.'

'There's more,' said Kent. 'There are rumours that your sisters are growing tired of having your father around. He divides his time between them and tries to give them advice, but they don't listen. There is talk that they are trying to get rid of him … permanently.'

Cordelia's hand covered her mouth in shock. Despite being banished, she still loved her father very much and did not want any harm to come to him.

'What should we do?' Cordelia asked.

'I am going back to England,' replied Kent. 'I will disguise myself as a servant. I still have friends who work for your father, so hopefully I can get close to him and help him without him recognising me.'

Cordelia nodded. 'Then I will speak to my husband. We will bring the French army to Dover. If we cannot get England back for my father, then at least we can try and rescue him before my sisters do anything to harm him.'

‘Here are your riding gloves, Your Majesty,’ said the servant, laying the gloves by Lear’s side and backing away.

‘Thank you,’ replied Lear. He was getting ready to ride to Goneril’s castle. His knights were already in place, ready to leave. ‘I have to say, you are one of the most accomplished servants I have ever had. And to think you have only been with me a few days. How did I ever manage without you?’

The Duke of Kent smiled behind his servant disguise.

'Thank you. Your Majesty is very kind,' he replied. 'My only wish is to help you, after all.'

Chapter Six

Goneril slammed her bedroom door behind her. 'I *cannot* take it any longer!' she screamed, making her husband, the Duke of Albany, look up from his writing desk in shock.

'What is it now, dear?' he asked.

'My stables are full of *his* knights' horses,' she said. 'The castle is crammed with *his* people. Dinner time is noisy and chaotic, and he will not stop trying to give me advice!'

Albany nodded his head. 'I presume we are talking about the old king, your father,' he said.

'Who else!' Goneril snapped. At that moment, there was a knock on the bedroom door and, without waiting for a reply, Lear himself walked in.

'Ah! There you are, daughter,' he said. 'I have some things I wish to discuss with you. These new taxes you have introduced, are they really necessary? They are making the poor even poorer!'

Goneril sighed and slumped down on her bed.

'And another thing,' Lear continued. 'One of my knights said that your stable boys aren't giving my horses much to eat!'

Suddenly, Goneril sat up straight. She glanced at Albany and smiled, as though she just had the most wonderful idea.

'Well, Father, there is a reason for that,' she said, standing and placing her hand comfortingly on Lear's arm. 'You see, you have so many *friends* who travel with you, it's hard to feed every person and every horse. That's why I had to raise the taxes to pay for your visits.'

Goneril winked at Albany. Of course, none of this was true. Goneril had raised taxes because she wanted more money. She had plenty of food stored away and enough hay for 500 extra horses, let alone one hundred.

'Oh dear,' said Lear, looking confused. 'I had no idea. What do you think we should do?'

Goneril grinned.

'Perhaps you could travel with only fifty knights, instead of one hundred,' she said.

Lear nodded slowly, scratching his chin in thought.

'Well, if you really think I should–'

'I do!' said Goneril quickly, as she guided her father through the door and out of her room. 'In fact, why don't you go and tell them now, before you leave to visit Regan?'

Lear allowed himself to be led out of Goneril's bedroom, and when the heavy wooden door was closed behind him, Goneril laughed with joy.

'That was so easy!' she said, clapping her hands in delight. 'The old fool will listen to anything I say!'

Albany was impressed with his wife's cunning lie.

‘Very clever, my dear,’ he said. ‘But your father still has fifty knights. That’s *a lot* of people on his side, ready to defend him.’

Goneril smiled again, reaching for the quill and ink on her bedside table.

‘Not for long!’ she said, as she began to write a letter to her sister.

Chapter Seven

Regan put down her sister's letter and jumped up from the table where she and her husband, the Duke of Cornwall, were having breakfast.

'Goneril has come up with a plan!' she said.

'For what?' asked Cornwall, looking up from his plate.

'To rid us of that troublesome

old king, my father! Look at this!'

Dearest sister,

You will be delighted to hear that my father has dismissed half of his knights – those troublesome men who follow him everywhere and act as though he is still in charge of the country. Now, you must do the same. Tell him you have no money to pay for his knights at all! He must get rid of everyone. That way, the only people left to defend him will be that silly old jester and his new servant. We will be in control at last!

'Isn't it a splendid plan?' Regan asked, as Cornwall finished reading the letter.

Cornwall put down his knife and fork. 'My dear, your sister seems to be obsessed with getting rid of your father,' he said.

'He interferes too much,' replied Regan, irritated. 'She wants to be in control of her own lands, just like I do.'

'Perhaps,' said Cornwall. 'But what will she do when Lear is out of the way? Do you think she will stop there?'

Regan frowned.

'What do you mean?' she asked.

'What if your sister means to take over all of England for herself?'

Lear watched as his knights left the stables at Regan's castle. As his last friend trotted away into the evening air, he hung his head and sighed sadly.

'Your Majesty,' said Kent, quietly. 'Is everything all right? May I fetch you something?'

Lear shook his head, miserably.

'They are gone. All gone. My trusted friends and protectors,' he said.

Kent tried to hide his anger. He knew, of course, exactly what

Goneril and Regan were up to. He had known them since they were little girls and had watched them grow into selfish, greedy women. He could not say anything to Lear, for fear of revealing who he truly was.

'What will you do now?' asked Kent, frowning.

Lear shook his head. 'I-I suppose I will go back inside and see my daughter,' he said. 'At least I still have two loyal daughters left.'

Lear trudged slowly back to the grand entrance of Regan's castle, but as he approached, there were no footmen to open the door for him.

He tried the large brass handle, but it did not move. He thumped his fist on the door, but there was no reply.

'Hello!' he cried. No answer came.

The castle was silent and locked tight.

Chapter Eight

The jester pushed a cart of supplies alongside the old king as he and his servant walked through the dark countryside.

'It's getting darker! The night's drawing in, but no knights to be seen!' the jester said in his sing-song voice. 'Poor old Lear left out in the cold!'

'Quiet!' said Kent, linking his

arm with Lear's to help him walk. 'You are not helping.'

'He has every right to make jokes,' said Lear, sadly. 'I have been a fool, and fools should have jokes told about them.'

Kent sighed.

'You are not a fool, Your Majesty,' he said.

'I must be!' replied Lear. 'My daughters were good and true, yet somehow they have turned against me. I must have done something terribly bad to make them behave that way.'

Kent realised the time had come. He had to reveal himself to the king.

'No, sir, that is not true,' he said. 'Your daughters have always been dishonest and unkind. I saw it from the very first day you decided to divide your kingdom.'

Lear looked at his servant with an expression of confusion spreading across his face.

'And how would you know that?' he said. 'You have only been my servant for a few weeks.'

Kent took off his servant's cloak and stood up tall and proud.

'The Duke of Kent! What a lark! He has returned even though you told him not to!' said the jester, skipping around Kent, laughing.

Lear took a step closer to Kent.

'Is ... is it really you?' he asked. 'My old friend who I treated so badly?'

Kent nodded.

'I am *still* your loyal friend, Your Majesty,' he said. 'And I have a message from Cordelia. She and the King of France have set sail to help you. They should be landing in Dover at any moment. They are ready to fight for you.'

Lear's eyes filled with happy,

grateful tears.

'You knew!' he said, happily. 'You knew it was really Cordelia who loved me the most! I have been so blind!'

The English Channel was dotted with a fleet of ships, bobbing up and down on the water. On the shore, Cordelia watched the horizon for any sign of her father and the Duke of Kent.

'They will be here,' said the King of France, kindly.

'I have missed my father so much,' Cordelia said. 'I only wish–' she stopped, spotting three figures walking towards them. 'It is them! They are here!'

Chapter Nine

As soon as Regan discovered that Cordelia and the King of France had arrived in England, she sent a messenger to her sister, Goneril. If they were to defeat their father and their troublesome little sister, they needed to work together.

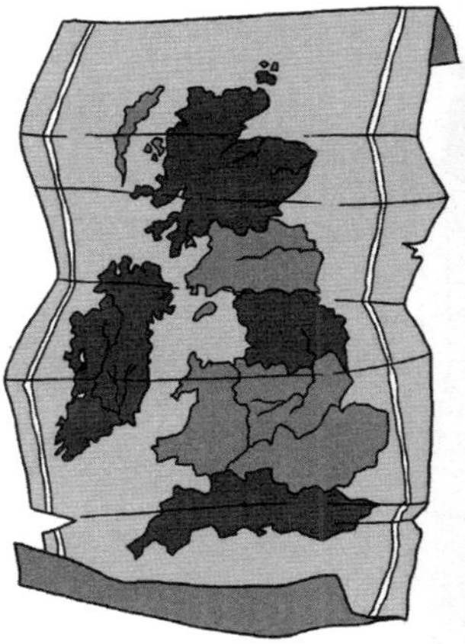

When Goneril arrived, the sisters talked late into the night.

They had each become so obsessed with their own power and greed that they argued about everything. From disagreements about how many soldiers to send, to where they should take their father and sister once they had captured them.

Finally, both sisters had had enough of snapping at each other and angrily walked away in disgust.

'I do not trust her!' said Goneril yet again, as she stomped around her room. 'Regan is clever and deceitful. I will need to watch myself or she will want to take over my half of England, too!'

'Isn't that exactly what you want to do to her?' said Albany, climbing into bed, weary of his wife's anger.

'Of course it is!' she said.

deceitful

Being dishonest or hiding the truth.

‘Then why don’t you try and do something to stop her,’ Albany said sleepily, his head gently hitting the pillow.

As her husband slept, Goneril’s mind spiralled deeper and deeper into dark thoughts. She had managed to get her father out of her way, and now it was her sister’s turn.

‘Sister? Are you awake?’ Goneril whispered in a sing-song voice through her sister’s bedroom door.

After a moment, Regan opened it and warily stepped out of her room.

'What do you want?' Regan replied, harshly.

'To say sorry,' Goneril said, handing her sister a mug filled with warm milk. 'I have brought you this to help you sleep.'

Regan took the cup and frowned at her sister.

'We must work together,' Regan said. 'Once Father and Cordelia are dealt with, we can argue all you like.'

Regan took a large sip of the warm milk, and the next instant an odd and terrified expression swept over Goneril's face.

'Regan, wait!' she said, suddenly snatching the cup from her sister's hands. 'Spit it out! I'm sorry! I should not have done it!'

But it was too late. Regan collapsed onto the floor, poisoned by her sister.

'What have I done?' Goneril said, sinking to her knees. 'What have I done!'

Chapter Ten

The Duke of Albany sat on his horse next to the Duke of Cornwall. Behind them, a troop of soldiers were ready to march into battle. They had travelled for days to reach Dover. Once they were there, they saw the French army camp, ready to invade England. They knew that somewhere among the tents and boats, Lear, the Duke of Kent and Cordelia were plotting.

'I am glad you came,' said Albany to Cornwall. 'After your wife's tragic death.'

Cornwall refused to look at him.

‘My wife was murdered,’ Cornwall said, sternly. ‘And I have a good idea who did it. But for now, I will carry out her wishes. She wanted to fight her sister and father, and drive them out of England. I will do that for her.’

Albany paused for a moment, unsure what to say. He suspected that it was Goneril who had poisoned Regan, but since that dreadful night, Goneril had refused to get out of bed. She cried and wailed. She could not sleep and muttered to herself in a kind of tormented daydream.

'Goneril has been very upset,' he said at last. 'I think the news has sent her into a delirious fever.'

delirious

To be unable to think or speak clearly because of mental confusion.

Cornwall stared at Albany, hatred in his eyes.

'Good,' he said at last. 'It is no more than she deserves.'

A flag was raised in the French camp, signalling that they were ready to fight. A huge roar was heard from the soldiers behind Albany and Cornwall as their horses surged forward into a gallop.

The battle had begun.

It was strange to hear the gentle lapping of the English Channel after so much noise and confusion. The battle had ended. A few French soldiers and the King of France had escaped. All that could be seen of them was their boat, now just a small dot on the horizon as it sailed back to France, defeated.

The victorious Albany wandered along the shoreline. His troops had captured Cordelia and Lear. He had done everything he had set out to do, and yet his victory felt empty. His thoughts kept returning to Goneril. How could she have killed her own sister?

At that moment, a young soldier approached, breaking Albany from his gloomy thoughts. The soldier held a small, folded piece of paper in his hand.

'A message from the Duke of Cornwall, sir,' he said.

Albany's eyes scanned the note. Goneril had died of her guilty fever. His heart thudded in his chest. Now that both his wife and Regan had died, he wondered who was left to rule over England?

His hands trembled as he quickly realised who the crown had now passed to.

Cordelia.

Cordelia, who he had just fought and captured, had now become Queen of England!

'You!' he said, calling back the soldier who had given him the message. 'We must go at once to where Cordelia and the old king are being held. We must tell them we have made a terrible mistake!'

Chapter Eleven

Cornwall stood outside an old, abandoned barn. His sword was drawn, ready to attack. The barn was being used to hold Cordelia and Lear before they could be taken to his castle to be imprisoned. He felt proud that he had been able to fulfil Regan's last wish and had decided to guard the prisoners himself.

Suddenly, Cornwall heard the thundering of horses' hooves as Albany and the young soldier arrived.

'Goneril is dead,' Albany said, dismounting his horse. 'They say

she died of a fever, but I suspect she died from guilt. You said as much yourself before the battle. Goneril killed Regan, I am sure of it.'

Cornwall stared in disbelief.

'But if Goneril and Regan are both dead, that means–!'

'Cordelia is queen!'

The men rushed to open the barn doors, to set their prisoners free, but instead they were greeted by a terrible sight.

Lear slowly walked towards

them with Cordelia slumped in his arms. Kent followed behind, his eyes red and his face streaked with tears. The jester came last, unable to lift his eyes from the ground.

'It is all my fault,' said Lear, gently

placing his daughter on the ground. 'My vanity and foolishness led to this battle. If it was not for me, my daughters would all still be alive.'

Cornwall and Albany looked at Cordelia. She had been brave enough to join in the battle, but it had come at a great cost. She had been wounded and had passed away in her father's arms.

'I know now that Cordelia loved me the most,' said Lear, tears falling from his eyes. 'She who could not say the words but felt the love more than anyone. What a fool I have been.'

Lear slumped beside Cordelia,

his body shaking with great heaving sobs until he could no longer take the strain. Lear, with no family or kingdom left to live for, died beside the daughter who had remained loyal to him right to the very end.